Infinite gratitude goes to the Source of all creation, for breathing Its Breath of Life into this vessel that is Elizabeth. Thank you also to Lisa Jane (www.lisajane.com) for allowing me to use one of her images within the composite of the front cover picture. Thank you also Lisa, for your encouragement for this book, and for your photographic art that was my friend during very difficult years.

I would also like to extend thanks to my publisher Bruce and his team, for all their effort and amazing support.

Thank you also Eddy for your love and support as well in this endeavour.

And to Sensei Jerry Wong, thank you for the energetic and spiritual influence in my life, as well as an amazing friendship.

Lastly, I want to thank Grandpa, Mom, dad and Niquey, for your loving influence during the creation of these letters.

Letters to Heaven

INTRODUCTION

There is a song called 'Higher', performed by the band Creed, written by Mark Tremonti and Scott Stapp. It's about being taken to a higher place within one's sleeping dreams, escaping the pain of this world while awake. It is a wish that their dreams could be what earth was like, if we could live from a place of Love instead of fear and hatred. It perfectly expressed my longing and hunger within for something better at that time, with a tune I love. I wish you could hear it right now. In fact, why don't you? Play the song on your device to feel the emotion before you start reading. And if you like the genre, buy it and support the artist :)

At a young age, after my foundations were ripped away more than once, I spent more than a decade making questionable choices because of my anger. In my 20's, I went after something I thought would bring all that I wanted, and crossed every line drawn in the sand by church and family to make it happen....and crashed, falling flat on my face. I contemplated suicide at one point, but chose not to, as I did not know if the grass would truly be greener on the other side. As loneliness and loss continued, my beloved grandpa died, taking me to an even deeper despair and guilt. I couldn't believe that this was it in life, that we love, and love hard, only to have it yanked away outside of our control. It did not compute. I could not accept it and something inside me was driven to rise higher, to seek the love I craved within my heart. I had to lean on a foundation that would not change, so something inside me was driven to rise higher, to find this love I so needed. I had to find some kind of meaning, or life just seemed a cruel joke. And so the letters to heaven were born, starting when Grandpa died. I chose to reach out to God for the love and companionship my soul craved, rather than plummet into full blown depression. I could not find it in the world I saw with my eyes, and since I would not give up on hope, I chose to reach out to forever. Something deep within knew a Love existed, one that could never be taken, one that transcended every pain. I took ever so seriously the promises I was taught about a loving Creator as a child, and brought them to life within my heart. I rose higher into a peace I never knew existed, and gained the freedom to love unconditionally as I no longer needed others to love me in order for myself to feel loved. This became a new foundation, and one that I have carried with me through a couple of more dark pits.

Although the letters were reaching outward at first, beyond the world I could see, the journey ultimately turned my attention inward, 'beyind' so to speak. I moved through my internal psychological conditioning of fear, and metaphorically it became the start of the caterpillar's journey in its search for the butterfly.   I learned that I was so much more than just a land bound creature tied to pain and fear, and that the world I saw with my eyes was not the end all of everything. There is a higher love, Agapé Love, that gave me wings of freedom to enjoy a peace that passes understanding here on earth. And it is not something you necessarily do, but rather allow first, then the doing follows. Once my intention in life became this loving outflow, all doubt, despair and fear began to slowly disappear.

It's been many years since I wrote these Letters to Heaven, and as I mentioned, life has taken me to the pit and back a couple more times since, each time deeper into darkness than the previous experience. I have returned to these letters each time, to draw me out of the darkness once again, and re-ground my being in God's Love.

It is my hope that offering this portion of my life as an open book, that it might awaken the 'butterfly' in others, the truth of who we are. I hope it inspires even one person to cultivate their own personal, unique relationship with the Source of all Creation, and discover true peace within the turmoil in our world, as forces endeavour to extinguish our light collectively. Or maybe someone will take it to a deeper level if that relationship already exists. Or maybe you will come and teach me this instead. Everything that I know I am, you are too! We all have experiences that pull the rug out from underneath us. Circumstances may be different, but the lessons learned are the same. May people choose to shine their light, regardless of external circumstances, and believe that we are so much more than we are told. We all possess something within ourselves that is so magnificent, so beyond what we can comprehend, but it is buried beneath many layers of fearful conditioning and programming. If one is ready to look 'beyind', to look inwardly beyond their fears, and the belief that we are separate from one another and all creation, they will find the Loving Presence that is connected to all life, the True Love that is <u>not</u> dependent on one's external environment, that Love which allows one to find contentment within discontent. It is the most important thing we can do right now; making the outflow of the Loving Source within, your intention in life. The Source that breathed Its breath into you at birth continues to do so to this very day, but most of us are asleep or 'dead' to that knowledge. You <u>are</u> the breath of God. Breathe it!! And begin to experience the journey of the pearl of great price, and by trading all your fear for this Higher Love! The practice of Agapé love is the ladder that takes us higher. And if life seems to be a roller coaster ride, taking you to the heights and back to the depths, be rest assured, no matter how many times you plummet, there is ALWAYS a way back up. Love is ALWAYS waiting to lift you again if you choose the journey of Love-olution (the evolution of Love in your heart). I know! I've lived it! 😄

Where it all began...

Dear Grandpa,

At times you seem so far away, and I feel so sad with the loss, but my sense of temporary loss is your eternal gain. Although it seems impossible, I will replace my thoughts of sadness and fear with love and trust in God; thoughts that you are in a perfect world, away from the pain, tears and pressures of this physical existence. I will endeavor to live the hope we have, trusting fully in its promise.

You are with the Lord now. Is it glorious? What is it like when your spirit is released from its physical prison, into unfettered communion with our Father? What is it like to be embraced by God? What is it like to be fused with forever? What is it like when Divine Love penetrates your innermost being? What is is like to return to truth?

We've come now to the end of our time together on earth, and I'd like to thank you once more for the love that you gave. To have known your unconditional love was to have had an insight into the depths of God's love for me. It helped bridge a gap in awareness of the love of our Father for His children. Even though I am taught that God is with me always, He becomes all the more real to me through your loving influence in my life, inspiring me to offer the same to others.

I hope that the loss of your physical presence will greatly enrich my life. Somehow Heaven seems closer, more real and attainable to me to know that you are there. If I didn't have the hope of one day seeing you again, knowing this separation was only temporary, I wouldn't be able to survive the loss of a loved one such as you.

Nothing can ever really keep us apart. Everything you modeled will be part of me always. I want to mirror to others in my life your unconditional love, your kindness, gentleness and patience. I want to help others feel as good about themselves as you did for me. You gave me self-worth and total acceptance. As I mirror these traits, you will always be alive in my life.

Dear Grandpa, our relationship has not ended. It has only changed. As physical death is only a transition of life, so is it also a transition of our relationship, because I believe you are still alive.

God must be glad to have you home. I bet if the size of your crown of life is gauged by the happiness and love you've given to me, it must be the size of Heaven.

Thank you for your legacy of love, Grandpa. I am so thankful for your example to follow. When my turn comes to meet the Lord, I hope that you and the rest of my loved ones who have preceded me or have yet to precede me in death, will meet me there, and accompany me across the threshold to eternal life. Until then, good-bye until we meet again!

With all the love possible,
Your granddaughter and sister in Christ,

Beth
PS, I soooooooooo miss you

<u>Dear God,</u>

Bring me back into Your light.
I have been lagging in the shadows of the world
with its burden upon my shoulders.

Release me Lord; take away my worry, pain and fear.
I need not fear anything
with Your tender and compassionate arms about me.

Love me Lord, and let Your strength and wisdom flow through
to me. Let Your wisdom become one with me.

There are so many beautiful things in this world.
Help me to focus on that which is lovely.

Thank You for all the influences and experiences in my life
that have led me back to You.

It is such a freedom to lean on something
that is everlasting and works no matter what.
How long will humans remain in ignorance and blindness?

The shadows are cold, dark, fearful, fleeting, inconsistent.
The light is the very opposite, radiating warmth and
brightness.

I don't know anyone who doesn't walk with a lighter heart
when the sun shines. Even the birds sing more in the sunshine.

Thank You for Your light. Draw me back into it, I pray!

Dear Papa,

You chose me to be made in Your image so that I could be Your daughter, to share in Your home as my father did his children.

Children should have a special place in the world of parents, so I guess it is the same with You.

I was born into Your family by my spiritual birth to partake of Your divine nature.

My father would always protect me, so You will too. Thank You for being my Heavenly Father.

♫ ♪♪♪

Guardian Angel,
protect the little child of
God.

Wrap her in your strong
wings of safety and
protection.

Encircle her with the love
and tender care
God has placed on you for
her.

She is the daughter of the
King,
and as such the Father God
has trusted you with her
care.

Protect the little child of
God, and keep her safe til
she comes home to the
Father.

♫ ♪♪♪

Written by Elizabeth Harris

<u>Ode to Keith Green</u>

Your music touches my soul.

It is a frequency that tunes my life to God.

Your music sings the song my soul wishes to express.

I cannot help but leave the pain of my existence far behind in the dust of my spirit's wake.

My soul reaches out of myself to touch the hand of the Father offered to me as your music draws Him near.

I inhale the spirit of your voice.

It delights our Father and Lord that you create a channel through which our spirits unite in love.

The medley of emotion, your devotion, adoration, humbleness and passion for the fullness of Christ rivals those which are my own.

Your words are alive, their spirit carrying me to the presence of God, where I am held, cradled and embraced.

Thank you for desiring to delight the Father and providing me a safety strap that would ultimately pull me back into joyful reunion with our Lord.

I can't wait to meet you in Heaven!

Searching for Jesus

Dear Jesus, sometimes I wish I knew more about your life on Earth. I wish I knew more about your struggles, your moments of deep despair and conflict. I wish the Bible had touched a little more on how you suffered, and how you overcame temptations. You became human to show us how a human could overcome.   Where are more of your humanly struggles?

Sometimes I wonder if it would help me to see more of your personal growth as a human. How deep did your struggles go? Where were more moments of growth, from spiritual infancy to spiritual maturity? I read of the outcome, but what did you go through to get there?

When I think of you as God, I get discouraged, because you had quite the advantage.. Sometimes I feel like I'm going crazy. I look to your example and all I have is the end result, not a whole lot that I can identify with. But I love you so much. I guess I love someone else more though, don't I? But their Heaven is my Hell and vice versa. So it's tough, really tough, and I don't feel godly because I'm so frustrated.

But Lord, you are truly becoming my dear friend and confidante more deeply through this. Take your rightful place in my life. Do what you must to remain unchallenged as the true and strongest desire of my heart, mind and soul. Strengthen my faith daily to trust in you always and completely, to never fear the unknown. Strengthen my faith to always trust and know that you did suffer many things, and always overcame. And although there are few examples, the common denominator in your victories was devotion to the Father's Truth and will.

Perhaps its doesn't matter what you suffered. We all suffer differently. I know you did, and you overcame the world.   And I know how now (..brown cow, haha..). Precious Jesus, Beloved Lamb of God, I love you so very, very (infinity more very's) much. And boy, if I can feel your love with such intensity, even with my physical barrier of a body, imagine when it's removed!!! 💞

Help me also to remember to lean on you when I can't overcome the world. You did, you will help! Thank you...for everything!

Forever and Always,   EG 💞

Holy Spirit, my spirit guide,

My heart hides in the shadows of guilt.

Shine the light of Abba, Father God, into
my darkness.

Embrace my being in His blanket of grace
and love, cradling this child of God.

Keep me centered in that comfort of
being, reminding me of who and what I
really am when life seeks to prove
otherwise.

My love touches Yours, my light illumined
by You.

Hand in hand with Jesus, we gather in
the presence of the Father to praise and
glorify Him.

Dear, dear Father in Heaven,

May I call You Daddy? It seems silly, but as I draw closer to You, sometimes the term 'Father' seems too formal. I use it still, as a more reverent way to address You, but somehow it still feels like there is a barrier. For me, to call You 'Daddy', denotes a bond of more intimate affection.

So Daddy :), let's embark on a new chapter of our journey together, a deeper level of intimacy. I love You soooooo much! You are the strength of my heart and my portion forever!!

Forever and Always, EG 💞

Darling little Jessica

*I give thanks to our Father in
Heaven for your little light
that shines. With my heart,
soul, strength and mind, I trust
this is part of His wonderful
plan.*

*A sweet fragrance you are.
Your soul is purity of life.
Unfettered by fear, untouched
by pain, your spirit unmarred
returns to the Father as pure as
the breath He exhaled.*

*Dear little angel, so very
special you are, that even
before your earthly life began,
your work in heaven was done
and the Father called you
home.*

*Precious little lamb, while your
parting grieves us so, it is but a
down payment for happiness to
come. You are safe in the arms
of the Father and one day we
will meet you there.*

******

For Jessica Ruth McGillivray

*Born February 6, 1998
Died February 5, 1998*

Dear Jesus,

Into your capable and loving arms I commit the spirit of Luthor. He is certainly going on to a better life. He was a good dog, no matter what happened in the end. Bottom line, it was our own faults. Dear Lord, use my guardian angel if necessary, to take him home to You. He is ever so loving and affectionate, and will be a wonderful companion for someone there. I did the best I could, and now Lord Jesus, please take care of the rest. My work with him is done (or perhaps his with me is done!). See to it that he is not lonely or sad, please? I doubt he could be there. Thank you for Your love and the love of our Father. Thank you Father for Your perfect working way.

Good-bye Luthor. I loved you as my own child. You were more than just a dog to me. You were my bud. You were a pal in times of loneliness and fear. You were what I needed during those difficult years on Simpson. You protected and befriended me. Do you, or can you ever understand what I had to do? Forgive me, my ever faithful puppy-pup, snoogly, snarfblast. You were so huggable, loveable, squooshy and cuddly. You craved the love and gave so much back, unconditionally and uncomplainingly. I hope I see you when I pass through death's doorway. Maybe you could also be there to escort me. There will never be another Luthor, my dear and precious dog. Even if I have other dogs, you will always be a special one. Maybe too you could go with my angel and continue to protect me. Please worship the Father on my behalf up there. Bow low before Him once for me, okay? Oh Luthor, you were so full of love, unconditional, never ending love. Surely that will not be wasted! Surely if an animal can have so much love, there's something special about it.

Take care, my dog! You have embarked (pun intended with teary smiles) on the next phase of your spiritual journey. Good-bye for now puppeee!! See ya when my turn comes!!

Forever and always,

Mommy!

Dear God,

Vacumming can be a real depressant. With a resolve to finally clean up and not wade through the dog hair on the stairs, I sadly began the task of sucking Luthor's dog hairs into oblivion. As I plugged the vacuum in, there were surges of hesitation and regret. I cried as I vacuumed. Each strand disappearing was like a fiber of my heart going with it. Luthor was continuing to vanish. Would people think me overly eccentric if I collected what remaining hair I could find and keep it in a special place? Some people keep locks of their kid's hair. Me, I just keep handfuls of dog hair. I suppose when Sears comes to maintain my washer and dryer, I'll have a fresh supply of dog hair stuck in all the nooks and crannies. I'm not expressing myself the way I'd hoped to. I wanted to be humorous but it still hurts so much. The pen knows! It hurt to watch the hair disappear. To just suck it back so quickly and impersonally seemed so callous. I kept saying "goodbye puppy". Yes, tears are flowing. I guess there are still a few painful times ahead. But a very kind thing came to my attention today. In memory of Luthor, our vets made a donation in his name to the Pet Trust fund at Ontario Vet College in Guelph. Yes, I burst into yet more tears. I grabbed my rottie stuffy and held tightly to it. I can still faintly smell my booboo on it. It's fading, though, like everything else.

Oh Father, I just can't believe he's gone! I just can't! It hurts so much! Is he with you? Is he alive somewhere? Where is he? Where is my baby? Oh God, please don't let love die! I just can't believe that a life that can love so unconditionally, courageously and affectionately could just die. Love like dogs are capable of just can't fade into nothing, can it? He used to wrap his paws around my shoulder. He could recognize expressions of affection between others and copy it. How can he be nothing special...just a dog...like so many say? How can 'nothing' love with a love closer to God than most humans can show? Luthor was wonderful. He was my outlet for giving and receiving lavishing affection. We had a real connection and could understand each other with only a look. Does it sound stupid to call him my child? He was, I raised him, nurtured him, trained him. I guess I don't have to convince you of any of this. I'm only really trying to convince myself I guess.

Oh, this has opened a fresh wave of grief. Oh Luthor, I wish I could hold you. I wish I could give you a big squooshy hug and roll your flabs of jowly loose face fur in my hands. Oh puppy, I miss you so badly!! Oh puppy, I just never anticipated anguish like this. God, I wish there were a way to talk to him. I can understand why some would seek a medium to contact a loved one. You ache for just a moment of contact, to know they still exist, an affirmation of your faith. You just need to hear them and feel their presence. It hurts so bad. Help me! Please help me! I don't know how to get through this! I feel so guilty. I feel like I killed him, like the way it was draining my spirit was the reason he was taken. And I should have stayed with him. He deserved that. Luthor, can you forgive me for being so weak? Father, can you? Somebody, please, help me!

"Blessed are those who mourn, for they will be comforted" Matt 5:4

Dear Father,

You have given me an incredible gift. You have comforted an anguish and soothed my pain by answering a prayer in a way I never imagined. I told You I had to hold him one more time, and while I didn't know how You'd do it, I knew You could. I had no doubt You'd find a way.

You allowed Luthor to penetrate my dreams. After the 2nd one, I realized what was happening and begged for one more chance. Thank you! You gave me my 3rd dream and this time I held my dog. I hugged him and hugged him and hugged him and squeezed him so tightly, just like I used to. You let me hold him again! For as long as I needed! Everything my heart and soul pleaded for happened, except telling him how sorry I was. I just held him and held him and held him. Thank you, thank you, thank you!!! I knew You'd find a way.

But this is such a roller coaster of emotions. The other night I was crying again for my loss, even after that wonderful dream. Oh Father, it's so hard to experience the death of one you loved as a child. The separation is so painful. You've experienced it, I guess, when Your creation "died" so to speak. Something you made, nurtured, loved and communed with directly separated themselves from You. Although anger was expressed, was it actually Your deep sorrow for that which was lost? Did You cry too? Even if one knows it will happen one day, it doesn't make it any less difficult to experience does it? Father, were You thankful for the time You did have with Adam and Eve in the garden? Did You value each moment? Was it exciting for You to watch mankind learn their baby steps?

Oh Father, I miss Luthor so much. He introduced me to You as an intimate friend. You were just an acquaintance before, just "God" to me. This giving of love seems to have brought us closer together. But will this pain ever go away? Well, I guess I can put it to good use. I said I'd make his death meaningful. Father, I love You. Thank you for allowing my puppy to visit my dreams. Thank you for my dog and the loving nature he brought into my life. He may not be made in Your image, but You are still his breath of life and there has to be a bit of You in him. How else could he love so much?

Dear Father,

Trying to suppress the grief of the past few months has been like trying to put a cap on an active volcano. Sometimes it makes the pressure stronger. But it's October now, and for the first time, I can finally begin to remember him and laugh. I still want to cry, but I can also laugh when I think of him. I was looking at various pictures at different moments of cuteness, and I remembered how he used to put his chin down on the edge of the bed, looking up at you as if to say "Whatcha doin'? How long can you ignore my cuteness for?" He certainly knew what to do to get mass quantities of love and affection. I laughed, wondering if he ever did that to anyone in Heaven. And then I got thinking about the afterlife of animals. As I enjoyed the moment of full confidence that Luthor was alive and well somewhere, drooling and being very cute, doubt began to slowly and quietly creep in and try to snatch my happiness away. And then I thought, so what! Nothing in the Bible says animals don't live on after death. They are even accountable for the lifeblood of man. It doesn't negate my salvation to believe that. They were important and worthy enough to be considered an appropriate offering for our mistakes, and they sure know how to love. They have the breath of life. What life breath is not of You? And what kind of pure love is not of You? And if I find out at my death that I'm completely wrong about this, considering the near death experiences of others, I won't really care at that point. I believe I will see Luthor again.

Dear Father,

A very special thing happened last night. Grant emailed me telling him of Luthor's communication to him. I cried, reading it. I had found a few stray dog hairs of Luthor's and held them in my fingers with one hand. I brought them to the palm of my other hand. Boy was the energy ever strong! My hand felt like it was pushing against jello. Images of Luthor became so real and alive in my mind, like he was there, right here, that I was overwhelmed with emotion. I cried tears of happiness and joy.

After that, after reading of Grant's dream and closure, I began contemplating and I realized the stronger the love, the stronger the energy and maybe that love is the fuel that not only propels this energy vehicle, but steers the wheel of thought in the right direction. I have been afraid to accept the idea that our loved ones are closer to us in death because it was just too good to be true. It is a great wish, but is it real? I'm not afraid anymore. I would hate to think I were holding anyone back, but if it were me in their shoes, but if I could spiritually help a physical loved one, even while I was physically dead, I'd do it! Our love would bond me to them. I would stay as long as necessary and then move on.

These are Grant's words exactly:

"Some things just can't be explained, only appreciated.

Closure - Dedicated to Luthor - the best friend God could offer to physically represent himself.

As I stared into the misty darkness, my own selfish fears arose and overtook my logical curiosity, and I shrank into a cowering ball, closing my eyes. I could hear it, breathing and pounding the ground, coming towards me. I dared not open my eyes for the fears within me overwhelmed me. Then it all stopped and for what seemed like an eternity I shivered in my fetal recline. When I finally found enough courage to open my eyes, I started to cry; it was what I had dreamed and hope of for so long. Luthor was there looking at me, perplexed by my emotional state. He was about 10 feet away and started to approach as if he was afraid but curious. Then I smiled through my tears and he bounded as quick as he could headlong, barreling me over and licking my face as if I had never lost him, and my heart was filled with a love which is unexplainable and not understood by those who have never experienced it. God had brought him back to me for a reason known to God and I, to renew my love to all creation, through an animal which had always given me unconditional, unrelenting love. An animal that in fact was a part of God himself, a true faithful friend that I had let down but somehow still retained a love for me stronger than anything I could explain in mere words. It was God and He loved me no matter what I had done."

*To anyone who asks me
the one thing they
should do with their life
(as someone did), I say:*

*"Be the child of God that
you are.*

*The rest will fall into
place"*

Paraphrase Matt 6:33

Beloved Creator and Source,

Thank you for allowing me to exhaust my perception of love on Earth, so that I could discover the Perfect Love of Heaven, in which there is no opposite.

Becoming disillusioned of my own doing, I lost sight of Love's true origin. It certainly is a need impressed upon our being isn't it? That much is evident by all the songs and poetry devoted to the longing and fulfillment of pure, perfect, infinite, unconditional love and acceptance. Seeking this externally, from others as imperfect as I, resulted in a deep discouragement with life. I guess, my Truest Soul Mate, that I have been trying to squeeze orange juice from elephants.

Love's origin is You. You authored it, planting its seed within my heart. It's Yours to begin with. You never intended that I find it within another, not this kind of Love. Tapping into something like this all-encompassing love is not to be found within the confines of separation alone, for that can so easily be turned into hate.

Dearest and Beloved, I no longer deny my hunger for this kind of Love. My longing comes from You, and I can never give up on it. I've been fashioned to experience Your indescribable ecstasies, and so I allow my perception of Love to be changed. I am Your child and I truly delight in You. I'm home at last, and my soul finds rest in You alone...

Loves fulfillment is You. It was brought to life in Christ and now I return it to You through the living presence of Christ in my life. Jesus sparked the flame and keeps it burning bright in my heart, where You reside.

And WOW!!! What results!! You shower love and grace from within, and the overflow pours out into the lives of others, for Your Love is too great to be contained within a single vessel.

My expectation has also changed. Opening to this outflow of Love from Its true source, rather than from my stagnant pool of fear and emptiness, has left me free to give to others freely and unconditionally. There is no longer a need for reciprocation, for the River of Your Love and Life in me constantly replenishes my soul.

I now know the only person I can change is myself. Dearest and Beloved, my soul has been set free by releasing others from filling a void only You can satisfy. Others will still bring love into my life, sometimes a little and sometimes a lot, but You, only You, can fill this deep well within.

Thank You so much for Your Living Water that will always quench the thirst of my soul. Truly, "Blessed are those whose strength is in You". Psalm 84:5

Forever and Always, EG

My precious Jesus,

I am coming back to you,
my first love.

What a tender reunion!

Lover of my soul, take your
place as commander of my
heart, that I may love others in
a like manner.

You have shown me my
weaknesses. Be my strength,
now and forever more.

I love you my friend.

May your presence and love
overwhelm my being so that I
am fed and filled by that alone.

Light my path my Lord. We
walk hand in hand again.
Thank you for your
ministering servants sent to
help me.

I love you, Jesus.

Forever and always, EG 💞

Precious Abba, Precious Friend,

You too call me friend

You shower me with love that transcends all human understanding

You are my Lover and my Friend. Wrap your arms around me. Cradle my head in your bosom. Wipe my tears with a whisper of love.

Come to my room of silence and talk to me. Enter my meditation.

Surround me with Your Presence until we are One in a Holy union. Hold me, whisper to me in the stillness of our joining. You are my true soul mate.

Walk hand in hand with me where'er I go.

Let my eyes only ever see You and how I may serve You in life.

Thank You for Your everlasting mercies and goodness.

Thank you for letting me into the holiest realm of friendship with You.

I will magnify You.

Our union will reflect off the mirror of my soul into friendship with others.

I will radiate Your Being, for without You, I am nothing.

Forever and always, EG 💕

John 4:24 "A time is coming and has now come
when true worshippers will worship the Father
in Spirit and Truth, for God is Spirit
and desires that we worship in Spirit."

Dear Father in Heaven,

I have sought a spiritual experience for my physical
eyes to see and physical ears to hear.

But You have shown me that spiritual experiences
happen every day.

Dwelling in You is a spiritual experience,
not to be seen with my body's eyes and ears,
but felt deeply within the heart,
the dwelling place of Your Holy Word.

By seeing Your Spirit in all things and in all
experiences,
every moment becomes a spiritual experience to be
revealed.

Precious Father,
draw me gently into this awareness
of Your Oneness in all creation,
by guiding me through the forest of my fears
which block Your light in my heart and soul.

..Thy Word have I restored in my heart,
that I may not live in separation from Thee. (Ps 119:11)

Forever and always, EG 💞

Ps 31:5a - "Into Your Hands I commit my spirit…"

God exhales and I live, preparing for death.

God inhales and I die, prepared for life.

I love You!

Forever and Always

EG

*I am a daughter of God and I love my Heavenly
Father.*

He rocks me to sleep and protects my slumber.

*He picks me up, swings me about, and I giggle with
delight.*

*When I am hurting, I cry on His lap. He comforts
me, cradling His little girl with tender love*

*When I am angry, He soothes me with soft words
and a gentle rebuke, tenderly diffusing my anger.*

*When I am lost and confused, He guides with
wisdom as a light to shine upon my path.*

*When I disobey, He patiently teaches me to learn
from my mistakes.*

As I do unto others and Him, so does He unto me.

*I am a daughter of God and I love my Heavenly
Father.*

Artwork by my mother, Mary Harris,

In praying for the faith to move mountains, the Lord revealed that the only mountain worth moving was the mountain that was me.

Precious Father, Creator Spirit,
we are united in Love.
You make my life your dwelling place.
May this structure be strong enough
to be indwelled by You.

I am Your 'souldier'.
Train me.

I bow in reverence before You,
To be Your child and friend.

Your arms are opened,
beckoning me to come enter your world,
that I may enjoy Heaven here on Earth,
and walk hand in hand with You.

Your Holy Spirit lifts me to Your
lofty heights.

May I always love the world as You Love me.

I love You, Papa.

Forever and always, EG 💞

*God's Love and Mercy
is the splint that sets
and mends a broken
life, the healing balm
for the wounds of our
ignorance, and the
cure for the disease of
separation.*

I once read somewhere that if God were omnipresent, that would mean there was nowhere that God was not, or God would not be omnipresent...

...What then is the separation...?

"Surely O God, you have worn me out; you have devastated my entire household…
Only a few short years will pass before I go on the journey of no return. My spirit is
broken, my days are cut short, the grave awaits me"   ~ Job 16:7,22 & 17:1

Daddy, help me!!!!!!!!!!!!

After a night of anguished sleeplessness, I feel like I've fallen down and can't get
back up. The above passage from Job was the first thing I opened my Bible to this
morning. A tad depressing, but certainly appropriate! O Father, I know that this
experience is one of Your refining fires of life. It hurts, it burns, it stings, and my
spirit feels parched and dry. But as much as I wallow in despair, You apply Your
healing balm as a provision to help me through. Thank you for these people. I must
choose to let them help, and I do. This is by far the closest I've come to walking
through fire. But as with the boys in the Bible, You go with me, protecting me from
the scorching flames.

I know You are purifying my spirit and I rise to the challenge. Again and again,
after each stumble, I will get up with Your help, dust the shit off and take another
step. Baby steps, right Father? I feel like I'm learning life all over again, learning to
think differently. I'm just a baby in Your arms. Babies only learn. They have no
clue of their ignorance. They just learn. It's harder as an adult to remember this.
It's difficult to unlearn fear and relearn that state of being endowed upon as a child.
Because I'm older now, I beat myself up for not knowing this, whatever 'this' is.
Learning to walk in spirit is like learning to walk when I was a baby. I'll fall many
times, but I'll always get back up and try again.

Ok…I'm ready. Take my hand and help me up and let's give it another shot. How
many more stumbles, Papa? I guess as many as it takes. Thank you for Your
unceasing devotion. I could not succeed without You. And thank you for teaching
me to be content with discontent, for therein lies Your peace.

Forever and Always, EG 💕

"He who dwells in the shelter of the most High will rest in the shadow of the
Almighty. I will say of the Lord, He is my refuge and my fortress, my God in whom
I trust. Because he loves Me, says the Lord, I will rescue him. I will protect him, for
he acknowledges my name. He will call upon me and I will answer him. I will be
with him in trouble. I will deliver him and honour him. With long life will I satisfy
him and show him my salvation."

~Psalm 91:1,2,14-16

Dearest and Beloved, Cause of all,

Yesterday was a bad day for me. It seems that my soul searches, of its own accord, for moments with You from my daily storehouse of thought and deed.

My soul cannot be nurtured by past memories, nor future dreams. It is only as I experience life here and now, in the present, that it is fed. And since I have been filling this storehouse with thoughts of worry and fear, how could I help but be anguished? I couldn't find You through the barrier of what did not exist. All I could find was the darkness I was filling my mind with. My soul panicked! My depression is really just a spiritual hungering for union with You. And by moving into my heart, I found You again.

Thank you, Heart of my heart, Love of my love, for giving me the eyes to see this with.

Forever and always, EG 💕

Dearest Father in Heaven,

Thank you so much for honoring my perseverance through this difficult time. As I write this, I realize that as I have persevered, so also do You. As I do unto others, I guess. I'm told that we have to wait until death for our heavenly rewards, but Father, You have given me heaven on earth. I don't know what lays ahead, but my Beloved, heart in heart with You I go. Onward, upward and inward, all the way!

I can face anything, now that I've found You within; found the butterfly within the caterpillar, the Kingdom of God within. Thank you for this! I cherish it and accept it with deep gratitude and promise to use it wisely. If I get sidetracked, as can happen haha, I know You will maneuver the rudders of my ship to steer me back on course.

It's not been easy to persevere. At the deepest darkest point, my pit experience, I held onto Your promises in faith, and thanked You (amidst a LOT of sobbing), for this experience, trusting You that it would lead to something meaningful. It was so hard to do, but I kept at it, repeating my thanks over and over and over (infinity more over's haha), like a mantra. Gradually I was able to begin to actually feel the gratitude, although it was only lip service to begin with. It becomes less difficult each time. I realize after time has passed, that giving thanks changed the direction of my thoughts from a downward spiral into darkness, into an outflow of Light from within.

Dear Father, I know not what lays ahead, and it is truly ok. I trust You, no matter how bleak it may seem. You have shown me, beyond a shadow of a doubt, that Your ways are ultimately the best, even when the short term seems dismal. But try and tell that to others who are in emotional anguish, eh? It's just one of those things you can only gain by experience and facilitating change for yourself. Ya know, I kinda feel like Disney's Cinderella when she was thanking her fairy godmother for the tremendous gift of going to the ball. Her gratitude is how I feel! But I don't need to tell You that! Our Spirit lives and breathes as One (most times I hope)

I love You, my Father, my Lord, my Hero and Friend

Forever and Always, EG 💕

Beside the river, within a forest, with flowers blowing lightly in the breeze, the Holy Spirit caresses my heart with His Gentle Breath upon the wind, bestowing kisses upon my being.

He massages my soul with the rippling water and speaks to all creation. They respond in unique song, each according to their kind. Together it is a symphony played for God, conducted by His Spirit's roaming whispers. I am its audience and participant.

It is here that I meet the Beloved and we share each other's heart. Oh what wonders Love can conceive! It is all that I can believe. Beauty and harmony as such cannot be found in another, but in the heart I share with the Lord it abounds. You are all that I can imagine, yet even more; you are the substance of infinity!

You alone possess the key, opening the door to eternity, where with you I can be. May I learn to recognize You by Your inner beauty, by that which is perceived with the senses of my heart. May I know You so intimately, that I recognize You in another, and bestow upon them the Love due You.

"In as much as you've done it to the least of My brethren, you've done it unto Me" ~ Matt 25:10

Sometimes in contemplation, I see life as a grand orchestra, each component being one of the various instruments that play the song of creation, composed by You, our Heavenly Father.

As diverse are the forms of life, so also are Your instruments in this great symphony.   Each is fashioned and tuned for a specific sound or effect.   Some have the lead while others are less frequently sounded.   Some are deep and quiet, while others are more lively and animated.   While all play a distinct melody and possess their own timing, as intended by You, they sound in harmonious balance.

The conductor is Divine Love, and the manuscript is Your Holy Word written upon our hearts.   The music is performed for our mutual pleasure, a song of rich beauty, because of our unified diversity.

Fine tune my soul, Dearest and Beloved, to sound its glorious song of Life.

Forever and Always,

EG 💕

♫ *Jesus loves me this I know,*

for our friendship tells me so.

All of us to him belong,

may be weak but he is strong.

Yes, I love Jesus. Yes, I love Jesus. Yes I love Jesus.

Our friendship tells me so.

I love Jesus every day,

in my sleep and in my play.

He is there where'er I roam.

Takes my hand and guides me home.

Yes, I love Jesus. Yes, I love Jesus. Yes, I love Jesus.

Our friendship tells him so ♫

Some revised lyrics by myself, but original lyrics
composed by Anna Bartlett Warner in 1860, and
tune by William Batchelder Bradbury, 1862

My dear Lord and friend Jesus,

My Beloved, thank you for guiding me to
Ste Therese of Lisieux. You have given me
a piece of Heaven by introducing us. I
carry her torch for you. Our love is one in
the same.

Thank you for you. I love you sooooooo
much! Rekindle the fire of our romance.
May I be content just to be with you.
Thank you for teaching me a deeper
spirituality and therefore a deeper
connection and communion with our
Father.

Like Ste Therese, I abide in Love. Love is
my vocation, my calling, my reward. Love
is my destiny, with you.

Forever and always, EG 💕

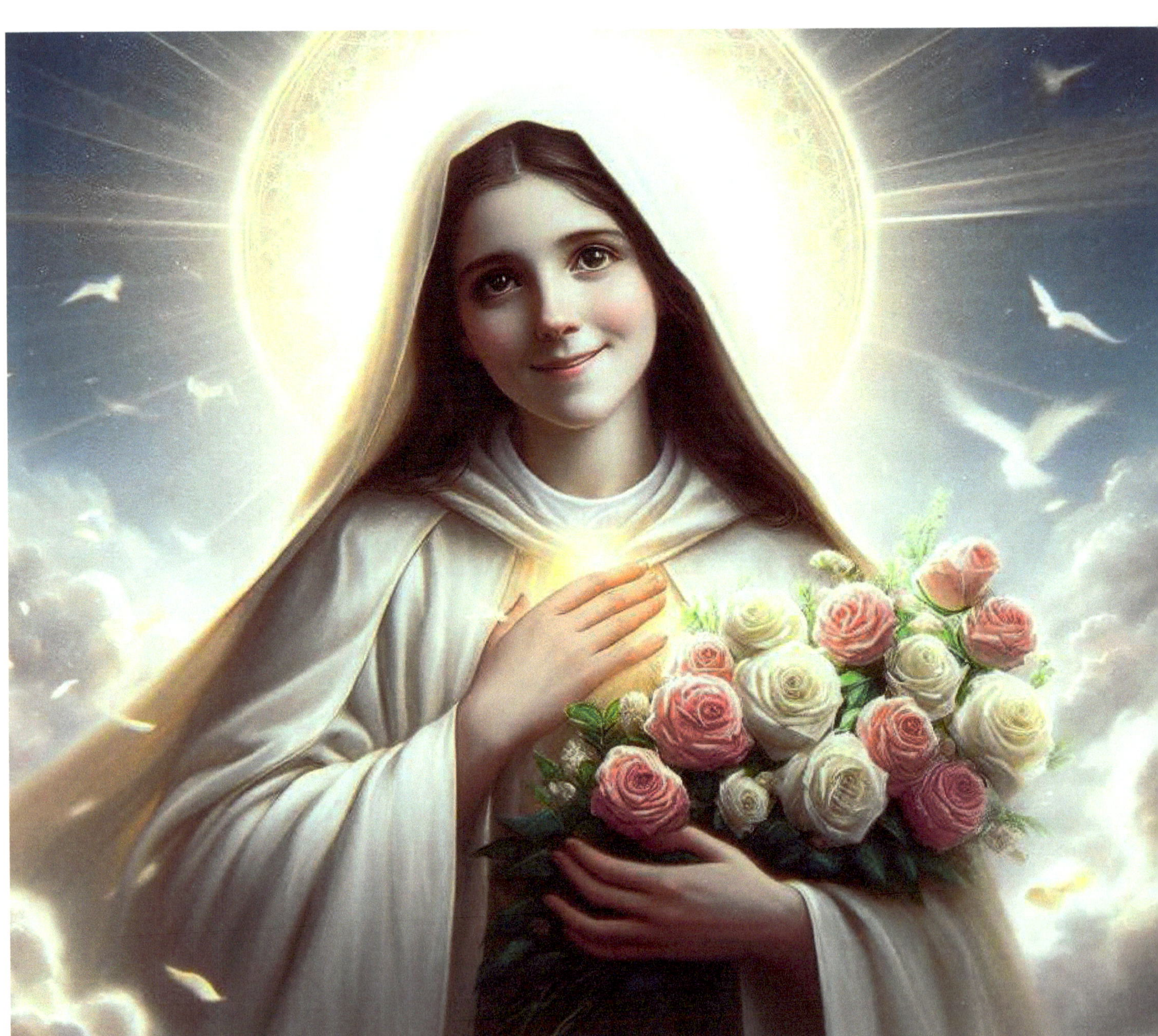

Ste Therese,

Meeting you has affirmed my worth in Heaven, to be just exactly who I am. Through your acquaintance, Jesus has shown me that just who I am, deep down inside, makes Heaven happy. I've spent most of my life trying to figure out what to do with it. I now know my path. It matters not how I do, but rather how I be. I've been so afraid to just be me, thinking I had to do something impressive to others. How could loving others like I love be a 'career'? Its my heavenly career here on earth I guess. Seeing myself reflected back as you in heaven's mirror says:

BE WHO YOU ARE BETH, IT'S WHAT HEAVEN WANTS. YOU ARE GIVING YOUR BEST, DOING YOUR BEST, BEING YOUR BEST BY BEING YOUR TRUE SELF, CHILD OF GOD. LOVE CAN DO ANYTHING. BUT LOVE. IT IS YOUR GIFT, ABOVE ANYTHING ELSE, LOVE! ITS WHAT YOU DO BEST. BE IT! BE LOVE! IT MATTERS NOT WHAT YOU DO. WE WILL DO, YOU JUST BE! BE THE CHILD OF GOD THAT YOU ARE AND THE REST WILL FALL INTO PLACE!

Thank you Ste Therese, for your influence and help. May Heaven help me live my being to its fullest!

Forever and always, EG 💞

Abba, Father of the Beloved,

I stand at the edge of a great chasm within my soul, looking across to You. Searching Your divine nature created a void in my innermost being. You nurtured and taught me, showering gifts from Heaven. Yet in the wonder of our friendship, there flickered a spark of haunting despair. Fueled by insecurity, the spark ignited, burning out the chasm I stand before today. But Your tender, gracious and loving way gently turned my heart around to look back and remember.

To truly love You is to love others. To be loved by You is to love others as You do, and that outflow of your Love that comes from 'beyind' me, (not from beyond ie, outside of myself, but rather deep within through the barrier of fear), flows into my being and out, for as I've said before, Your Love is too great to be contained within a single vessel.

Our beloved Jesus will close the chasm. He will reinforce our Souls bond by weaving them together with others. He will elevate our relationship to an even deeper dimension of Love. Teach me to truly Love and be Loved. In all my endeavors, may I only see them as loving You.

Forever and always, EG 💕

Dear Father,

I have always looked to others to pattern my relationship with You. Now you are making it ours. You have given me back to myself, which I now give to You. It always seemed a prideful thing to draw comfort, solace and inspiration from my own writings, yet those are the words Your Spirit has whispered in my heart. How could I not be strengthened by them? How could they not touch cords of hope and love within, as they are Your words to begin with. Might they help others too, Father? I have to leave that up to You.

But it is time to shine the Light You give, for glory only and ever, always to You. I no longer despair that my life has been wasted. I have a specific task — to Love. It's all I've ever wanted to do. Thank you for teaching to draw upon Your storehouses of Love, and not my reserves of fear. Remove fear from my life Father, for when fear moves out, Love moves in.

Do your thing, Daddy!

Forever and always, EG 💕

My Beloved Friend Jesus,

How my spirit leaps for joy at the thought of your name in my heart. My being is flooded with indescribable love and wonder. You, the savior of this ever expanding universe really and actually know me personally! At times I've wondered how you could be in so many places at once, when so many call on or talk with you every moment of every day. I feel selfish when I call on you so frequently, figuring someone else needs you more than I. But you don't work in time do you? So I will stop worrying about that, for the worry weights my soul, keeping it locked in chains of guilt and unworthiness. Somehow you have a way to do this :) While I don't know the inner workings right now, it is enough to just trust that it is so.

Thank you for sharing little gems here and there. Faith in you is the simplest way to go. It sure didn't seem like it at first, but I hung in and persevered through some really dark moments where I sobbed in despair, yet thanked you anyway for what you were doing through this experience. Gradually the weights are dropping, giving way to an incredible lightness of being. Thank you Jesus, for lightening my load.

Forever and always, EG 💞

Most precious Heavenly Father,

The first time I read the phrase "time meets eternity in the present", it struck such a chord within. By living the guilt of the past, projecting that weight into the future, I was just a dead weight. Jesus speaks of living for today. There's a lot to this, isn't there, Father? The present never ends, does it? It is never not now. And while we dwell within time, it's the closest thing to feeling eternity within my heart. Living within the present throughout this finite existence gives me a taste of the infinite and eternity.

Dearest most lovingest Daddy, help me live in the present. It's where I find You. I love you so much. And I miss You too sometimes. Things have changed, and I forget You are there, regardless of where my focus has to be. I got spoiled for a while, having You all to myself, with no other distractions. But this is necessary, and they are a part of life. So help me bring You more into the present moment no matter what is going on. And when something comes up, may You be the first thing my mind jumps to :).

Forever and always, EG 💕

PS, would it be a sin to smash the tv? Vous comprenez, haha

My Lord once said that

before I judge the speck in my brother's

eye, to first remove the plank

from my own.

I wonder, is the plank

in my brother's eye really

just the tip of the plank sticking out my

own eye, and when its removed, it will

naturally remove the speck I see in

someone else's?

Dearest and Beloved,

Several Christmases ago, I
was given 2 metal butterflies
of vivid color. It was
excitedly explained to me that
these colors were not painted
on the metal. Rather,
the deep shades were brought
from the colourless
metal by applying heat to
them. The longer
it endured the heat, the
brighter the
colors within were revealed.

It reminded me of
the refining fires we endure in
life. If we let them, they will
turn us into gold, and reveal
the true colour of our soul
within.

Forever and always, EG 💕

"…I tell you the truth, unless one is born again, he cannot see the Kingdom…You must be born again. The wind blows where it pleases. You hear its sound, but you cannot tell from where it comes or goes. So it is with everyone born of Spirit." John 3:3,7,8

Dearest and Beloved,

Is the language of Your Spirit like the
language of the wind?

The wind whispers through the leaves,
bestowing on each its tender kiss.

As the leaves respond to its touch, their
varied textures of dialect sing out their
brilliant song.

The wind speaks in Oneness, and in that
Oneness leaves give their unified
response in a diversity of song.

I would be like a leaf who freely sings the
melody Your Spirit whispers through my
heart.

Forever and Always, EG 💞

Dearest and Beloved,

Is the language of Your Spirit like the language of the wind?

Sometimes the wind is still.

Flora waits in restful repose for its next instruction while she quietly digests her nourishment thus far.

Without its voice, she does not make a move.

Yet, when once again the wind whispers through her, she sighs in blessed relief and continues her song.

I would be like flora, quietly meditating on your nourishment thus far, and lovingly anticipate your Spirit's next direction.

Forever and Always, EG 💕

Dearest and Beloved,

Is the language
of Your Spirit like the
language of the wind?

Trees sense the wind and
respond in unique song.

Their kind is many,
yet each praises
the same affection
whispered in their heart.

I would be like a tree,
standing firmly rooted
to hear the murmurs
of Your Spirit,
my life propelled by Its
flow and movement
through soul.

Forever and Always, EG💕

Dearest and Beloved,

Is the language of Your Spirit like the language of the wind?

A willow tree, planted by the banks of a river, is nourished by the constant watering of its roots.

While firmly grounded in its being, its branches sway unhesitatingly to the slightest whisper of the wind.

It cannot resist responding to the quietest murmur of a gentle breeze.

May I learn the lesson of the willow by being firmly planted and nourished by the streams of Living Water, yet ever so sensitive to the movement of your Spirit through my soul.

Forever and Always, EG 💕

Most Holy Creator,

Is the language of Your Spirit like the language of the wind?

Sometimes the wind blows in torrents unimaginable, toppling the largest of trees. Yet the tenderest reed survives un-maimed.

May my mind be as flexible as a reed, that I may survive the raging storms of life.

Forever and Always,
EG 💞

Dear Papa,

Walking my doggy this morning, ohhhhh...what a time! What a lovely few moments! As I walked, my eyes that see and ears that hear began to open. I looked at the snow on the ground, and guess what! I felt the One-ity! It was a recognition of Your Life Force, inherent in all things. Your Spirit breathes life into me, and it is the same breath of creation that gives existence to snow.

Father, when You thought about creating snow, did You envision all the little sparkles? Did you picture the beauty of new fallen snow on a bright moonlit night? As I pondered this further, it occurred to me that maybe if snow contained the same creative force as me, maybe it could tell me something about You also.

So, Dear Father, what do You teach when You reveal Yourself as snow? The snow spoke, saying:

"Look at the expanse before you. I am one covering, but many flakes, each an individual expression of being. I also speak to the One-ity of this existence. The many compose the whole, and the whole is comprised of the many. I cover the grass and dirt, the live trees and dead trees.   I am not partial to where I lay my blanket down."

Walking along I stopped thinking, and just wandered through the awe of this experience, absorbing the lesson into my heart with no analysis, no nothing, save the wonderment of a child.   At times it felt like my soul would shoot upward out of my body, in an unspeakable glorious ecstasy of being, leaving the form that drew a line through infinite Oneness in a heap on the ground.   Your Life, Your Spirit, was in each step I took no matter where these feet took me.

Thank you, my dear Papa. I love you!

Forever and always

EG

*Today I gazed toward the sun and said,
"Speak to me of Father Creator's Son." It
replied,*

*"I am the Light of your world. My radiance
feeds creation. It cannot exist without me.*

*Sometimes my brightness is concealed when
the back of your world is turned, but I am
always shining, ready to illuminate the
countenance turned back to face me.*

*Sometimes My Light is diffused by clouds,
but still I blaze as brightly as I was made to.*

*Even in the seeming darkness, My Light can
be captured by the reflective hope of the
dark rock in your sky, a reminder that my
presence is always there, even when the
back of your world is turned to me.*

*Tears of the firmament settle in melancholy
mist, blanketing your world in fog after
darkness. But when once more the face of
your world turns back to gaze at me, the
mists melt away to reveal the glory and
splendor, the dawning of a new day and
hope.*

*I am the Light of your world, and I will
always shine for you."*

Hello my Dearest and Beloved. I had a small maple sprouting in my garden, which I always pulled, but could never get it out at the root, so it just kept growing back, making the roots go deeper.

One day I finally got serious about removing it and with a small hand shovel, I began to gently dig the dirt away around it. I tried to pull it again but it would not budge, so I continued to dig. As I cleared more of the soil away, I could see that the stalk was getting thicker the deeper I went. I had a bigger problem than I realized, so I got a bigger shovel.

I eventually saw that the maple key's roots were wrapped around the roots of a bush I wanted to keep, so I had to work painstakingly slow and dig around it all so as not to harm what was worth keeping. Because of all the yanking I'd done at a surface level, the roots had grown deep and strong.

It reminded me of the negative aspects and habits of my life, mental patterns of thinking so ingrained and rooted within, that they required a painful and arduous excavation and extraction. Something so deeply rooted in my life cannot always be stopped at a surface level, requiring a deeper level of attention to expose more of the causes. I guess some things I think are a non-issue go far deeper than I realize.

Ultimately, after digging about a foot down into tough clay, enough of the root was exposed and I could pull it out. Although tendrils of fine newer shoots remained, it wasn't enough to be sustained on its own, and would disintegrate in time. This would be just like getting to the root cause of my own personal issues. Once unmasked, any residual emotion is no longer connected to its source, and thus begins to disintegrate too. Thank you for this my Love!

Forever and always, EG 💕

Dearest and Beloved,

Let us sit within the still and quiet waters of our Love.

Illuminate Your Spirit in this stillness of mind, indwelling within as restful repose, on the other side of the veil.

Beloved, just be, and I'll just be. Together we'll be. Let us bathe our Spirit in Love and intimacy.

I love you with all the love I have in my heart, and rest in Your arms of peace on the other side of forever.

Forever and always, EG 💕

Beloved,

You have come alive in my heart. You have
always been there , but now I understand
a little more the fluttering of the wings
of Your Soul as One with mine.

It took a deeper place of darkness to know a
deeper place of light, and oh how our Soul
dances in the joyous ecstasy of this deeper
union.

In that heart space of One-ity, the Life force
dances and I play within Its field , blowing it
out in kisses to the world around me.

And the more kisses I blow, the stronger is
your flow, deliriously happy that It has
found yet another open heart through which
to bestow dancing spirals of living love to a
hungry world.

Be alive in me! Take it to the limit, my Love

Forever and always, EG 💗

"I pray that they will all be one, just as you
and I are one—as you are in me, Father, and
I am in you. And may they be in us so that
the world will believe you sent me. I have
given them the glory you gave me, so they
may be one as we are one." ~John 17:21-24

The Union of St Symeon, the New Theologian

"We awaken in Christ's body as Christ awakens in our bodies, and my poor hand is Christ. He enters my foot and is infinitely me. I move my hand, and wonderfully my hand becomes Christ, becomes all of Him (for God is indivisibly whole, seamless in His Godhood). I move my foot, and at once He appears like a flash of lightning! Do my words seem blasphemous? Then open your heart to Him, and let yourself receive the One who is opening to you so deeply. For if we genuinely love Him, we wake inside Christ's body, where all our body, all over, every most hidden part of it, is realized in joy as Him. He makes us utterly real, and everything that is hurt, everything that seemed to us dark, harsh, shameful, maimed, ugly, irreparably damaged, is in Him transformed, and all is recognized as whole, as lovely, and radiant in His light. We awaken as the Beloved in every last part of our body."

Written by St. Symeon, the New Theologian,
who lived from 949-1022 AD

Dear Papa,

It would appear that you might be using a different strength or composition of fertilizer in my secret garden. It's almost like there were foundational nutrients that enriched the soil wherein the seed could sprout, but now we're moving onto to the food that supports the growing seedling of the flower about to emerge. I understand. Thank you for only ever breathing loving little breaths of holy understanding and guidance into my adolescent lungs of spirit. Bring my budding flower into full bloom.

Forever and Always,

EG 💗

My Papa, Beloved One,

Enter my perception and dissipate the clouds with the brilliance of Your Illumination.

Deliver me from the illusion of ego and wake me from this dream.

Hold me in Your arms as I awake into the Reality of You! I want to wake up!

Your loving child,

EG 💗

"Wake up, sleeper, rise from the dead, and Christ will shine on you."
~~Ephesians 5:14

Beloved,

At this moment now, I don't know what to call you. I feel like traditional names and titles are not enough to express what I feel inside. I feel as if I'm catapulted into Your presence because of the beauty I saw tonight. It showed me the wonder and beauty of our Love. It almost demeans it to even attempt to describe it in words. I can feel what I want to say, but there are no words for it. That's why watching this movie tonight really hit a chord DEEP inside. I felt like you were that secret love. Should such beauty as Our Love possesses be kept hidden? I guess maybe that's why I started my letters to you so many years back now. How do I put this emotion into words? I leave that up to you my Love. Where do we go from here? I feel like something's new, an added element of depth. We will discover each other together, hand in hand, heart in heart. I am awestruck!

Forever and Always, EG 💗

"Ask and it will be given to you; seek and you will find; knock and the door will be opened to you" ~~Matt 7:7

The Wall   ♫ ♪♪

I'm woven in a fantasy.
I can't believe the things I see.
The path that I have chosen now
has led me to a wall,
and with each passing day,
I feel a little more like something
dear was lost.

It rises now before me,
a dark and silent barrier
between all I am and all that I
was ever meant to be.
It's just a travesty, towering,
marking off the boundaries
my spirit would erase.

To pass beyond is what I seek.
I fear that I may be too weak.
And those are few
who've seen it through,
to glimpse the other side.
The Promised Land is waiting
like a maiden that is soon to be a
bride.

The moment is a masterpiece,
the weight of indecision's
in the air standing there,
the symbol and the sum of all
that's me. It's just a travesty,
towering, blocking out the light
and blinding me. I want to see.

Gold and diamonds cast a spell.
It's not for me I know it well.
The riches that I seek are
waiting on the other side.
There's more than I can
measure in the treasure of the
Love that I can find.

And though it's always been
with me, I must tear down the
wall and let it be,
all I am and all that I was ever
meant to be in harmony,
shining true and smiling back
at those who wait to cross.
There is no loss.

~~*Kerry Livgren**

♫ ♪♪

My Beloved,

I am ready.

Show me Divine Love.

Transform my mind.

Bring the Holy Spirit into my being, or rather
awaken it from within and let us dance!

And in the words of the poet Kabir, I say:

'Awake, my heart, Your master is near. Run to the
Beloved. So close by your drowsy head, having
slept for ages without number. Isn't this the
morning to wake up?"

Kiss me, my Beloved, and rouse the sleeping beauty
this day

Forever and always, EG 💗

My soul awakes!

It's first steps it takes, a moment forever embedded in Spirit!

All Heaven rejoices with Abba the Father and beckon the child come, to life immortal, happiness eternal, and peace everlasting as One.

This child is me, and O may I see the life that is promised in Thee!

Forever and Always,

EG 💗

"Do not conform to the pattern of this world, but be transformed by the renewing of your mind…." Romans 12:2a

I am Spirit;

I move with the wind.

*Where it blows I do
not know, but where
it leads me I will go.*

*That is its nature, not
bound by wants, save
the desire for Spirit
Itself.*

*I am a child of God
and it has fallen into
place.*

EG 

<u>*OUTRO*</u>

"The Kingdom of Heaven is within you" ~ Luke 17:21

"Very truly I tell you, no one can see the Kingdom of God unless they are born again" ~ John 3:3

"Wake up O sleeper, and rise from the dead and Christ will shine His light through you" ~ Eph 5:14

"Again, the Kingdom of Heaven is like a merchant looking for fine pearls. When he found one of great value, he went away and sold everything he had and bought it."
Matt 13:45-46

I pray that you will discover the truth of who you really are, and fly with forever. May you see the world through the eyes of Christ, and feel the knowledge of His Presence dance within the very cells of your body! May the peace of Christ be with you!